Judy Ann Sadler wrote the words
and Vigg drew the pictures, but ...

NOTHING HAPPENS IN THIS BOOK

published by Kids Can Press

This book looks boring, doesn't it?

You might as well stick it back on the shelf. Or toss it under your bed.

You don't need to read it because it looks like nothing happens in this book.

I'll bet the next page is blank, too.

See? What did I tell you!

Nothing happens in this book.
Just close it now!

Yes! A striped ball!
But no one is bouncing it.

This is a really shiny shoe.
But no one is walking in it ...

Hmm.
Here's a bright-red nose.
But no one is wearing it.

Hey! A trumpet!
But no one is trumpeting.

And a tiny car —
but no one is driving it.

Is anything going to happen
in this book?

There's a gigantic baton on this page, but no one is twirling it.

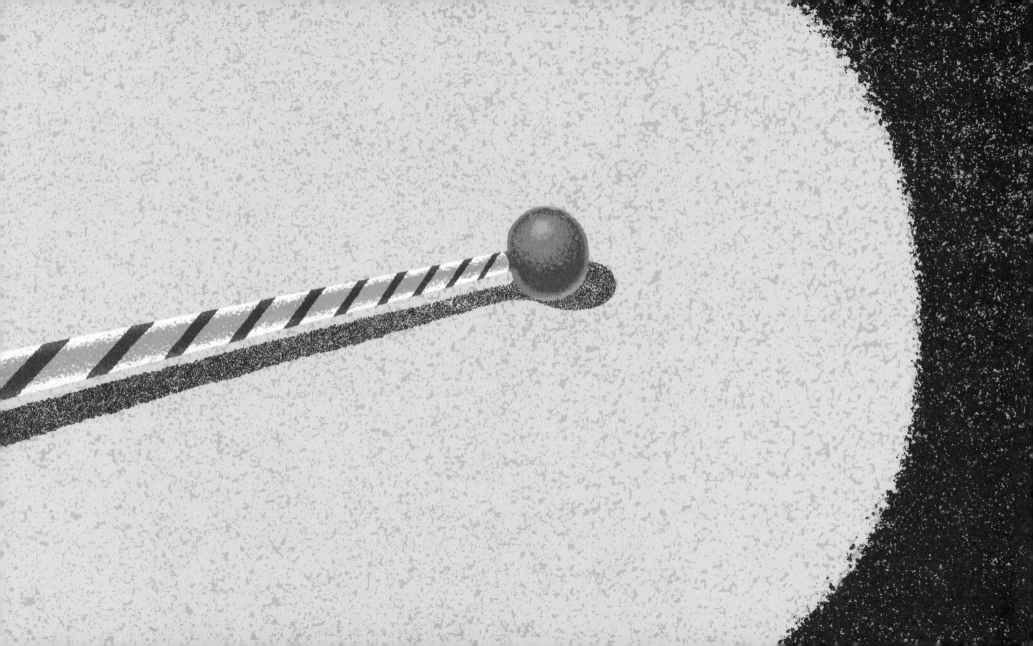

Here's a flag, but no one is waving it.

Oh! Balloons —
I better grab them!

Come on! Let's keep going!
Maybe something
will happen in
this book!

Cool, a crown!
A unicycle!
Uh-oh. Is that
teddy bear lost?

And I don't know what this is,
but it looks like fun.

This is a lot of stuff ...
I better get my wagon.
Meet me on the next page!

Look —
confetti!

And streamers!
And popcorn!

Something *must*
happen in this book.

Listen —
do you hear music?

I think it's coming
from the next page!

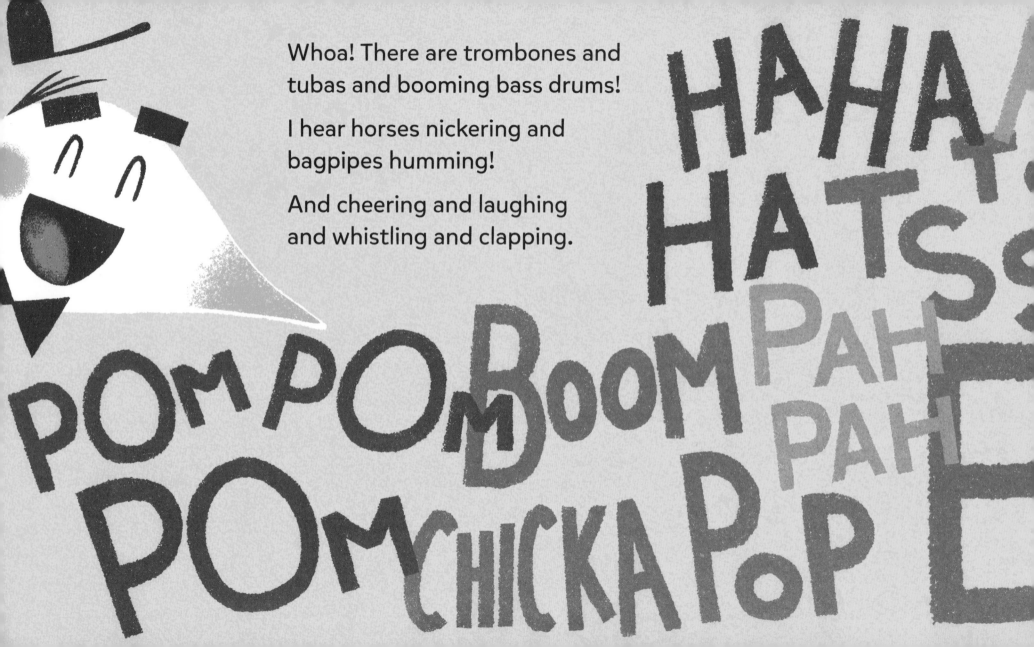

Whoa! There are trombones and tubas and booming bass drums!

I hear horses nickering and bagpipes humming!

And cheering and laughing and whistling and clapping.

HAHA

HATS

POM POM POM BOOM PAH PAH PAH

POM CHICKA POP

Aha! Something definitely happens in this book. And we can help make it happen.

I found your other shoe.

Well, good thing!
I've worn a hole
in my sock!

Here's your nose.

You can keep it.
My nose is already red—
ACHOOO!

Hmm. The marshal
doesn't look ready.

Oh, I know what the trouble is!

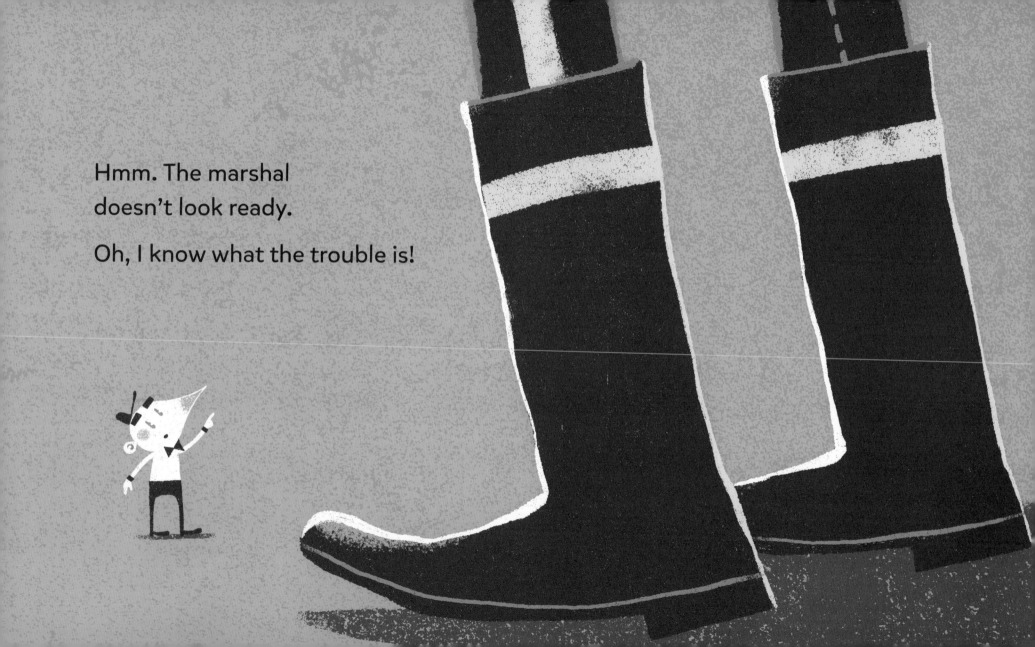

I knew this unicycle would come in handy! Come on!

WOW!

EVERYTHING HAPPENS IN THIS BOOK!

To Leo and Nash,
who are everything

J.A.S.

For Marianne

V.

Kids Can Press gratefully acknowledges the financial support of the Government of Ontario, through the Ontario Media Development Corporation; the Ontario Arts Council; the Canada Council for the Arts; and the Government of Canada, through the CBF, for our publishing activity.

Published in Canada and the U.S. by Kids Can Press Ltd.
25 Dockside Drive, Toronto, ON M5A 0B5

Kids Can Press is a Corus Entertainment Inc. company

www.kidscanpress.com

The artwork in this book was hand drawn and rendered digitally.
The text is set in Mikado.

Edited by Yvette Ghione
Designed by Karen Powers

Printed and bound in Shenzhen, China, in 10/2017 by C & C Offset

CM 18 0 9 8 7 6 5 4 3 2 1

Library and Archives Canada Cataloguing in Publication

Sadler, Judy Ann, author
    Nothing happens in this book / written by Judy Ann Sadler ; illustrated by Vigg.

 ISBN 978-1-77138-737-8 (hardcover)

    I. Vigg, illustrator II. Title.

PS8587.A2394N68 2018   jC813'.6
C2017-903828-1

Judy Ann Sadler is the bestselling author of more than twenty books for children. She lives in London, Ontario.

Vigg has written and illustrated several children's books as part of the creative duo Bellebrute. He lives in Montreal, Quebec.